JON SCIESZKA'S TRUCKTOWN
MELVIN'S VALENTINE

WRITTEN BY JON SCIESZKA

CHARACTERS AND ENVIRONMENTS DEVELOPED BY THE

dESIGN garage

DAVID SHANNON   **LOREN LONG**   **DAVID GORDON**

ILLUSTRATION CREW:

Executive producer: TOr INDUSTRIES in association with Animagic S.L.

Creative supervisor: Nina Rappaport Brown ◦ Drawings by: Juan Pablo Navas ◦ Color by: Antonio Reyna

Color assistant: Gabriela Lazbal ◦ Art director: Karin Paprocki

Ready-to-Read

Simon Spotlight
New York   London   Toronto   Sydney   New Delhi

SIMON SPOTLIGHT

An imprint of Simon & Schuster Children's Publishing Division

1230 Avenue of the Americas, New York, New York 10020

Text and illustrations copyright © 2009 by JRS Worldwide, LLC.

SIMON SPOTLIGHT, READY-TO-READ, and colophon

are registered trademarks of Simon & Schuster, Inc.

TRUCKTOWN and JON SCIESZKA'S TRUCKTOWN and design

are trademarks of JRS Worldwide, LLC.

For information about special discounts for bulk purchases,

please contact Simon & Schuster Special Sales at 1-866-506-1949 or business@simonandschuster.com.

The Simon & Schuster Speakers Bureau can bring authors to your live event.

For more information or to book an event contact the Simon & Schuster Speakers Bureau

at 1-866-248-3049 or visit our website at www.simonspeakers.com.

The text of this book was set in Truck King. / Manufactured in the United States of America

0115 LAK / First Simon Spotlight edition / 10 9 8 7 6 5 4 3 2

Library of Congress Cataloging-in-Publication Data / Scieszka, Jon.

Melvin's Valentine / written by Jon Scieszka ; characters and environments developed by the Design Garage ;

drawings by Juan Pablo Navas ; color by Antonio Reyna / p. cm.—(Trucktown. Ready-to-roll.)

Summary: Melvin the cement mixer worries when he cannot figure out who gave him a valentine.

[1. Trucks—Fiction. 2. Worry—Fiction. 3. Valentines—Fiction.] I. Design Garage. II. Title. / PZ7.S41267 Mh 2010

[E]—dc22 / 2008030723

ISBN 978-1-4814-1458-6 (hc)

ISBN 978-1-4169-4144-6 (pbk)

Melvin got a valentine.

But he did not know
who it was from.

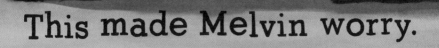

This made Melvin worry.

Melvin asked Kat,
"Did you give me
this valentine?"

"No," said Kat.
"But it is **Pretty.**"

This made Melvin
worry more.

"Beep, beep."
Rita laughed.

"Jack, did you give me this valentine?"

"Nope," said Jack.

This made Melvin worry
even more.

"Beep, beep."
Rita laughed.

Melvin asked everyone,
"Did you give me
the valentine?"

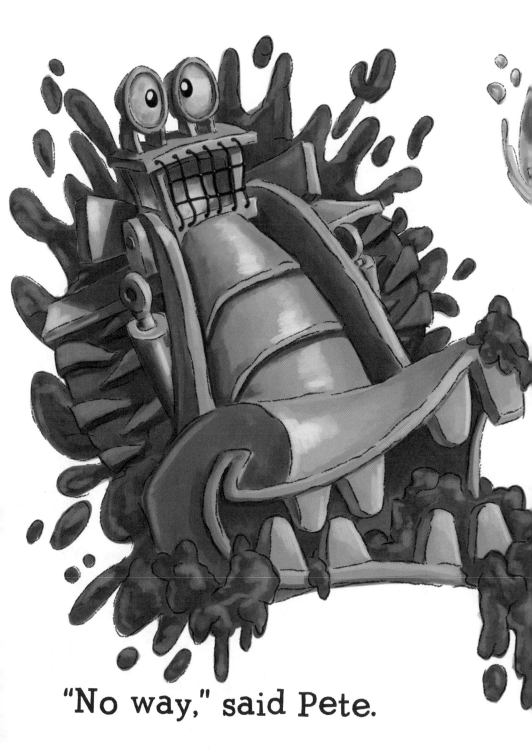

"No way," said Pete.

"Not me," said Lucy.

"Not me," said Pat.

Melvin was really worried.

"Beep, beep," Rita called.

"Hey, Melvin," said Rita.
"I am so glad you showed
everyone my valentine."

"YOUR valentine?"
said Melvin.

"Oh. I am so glad too."

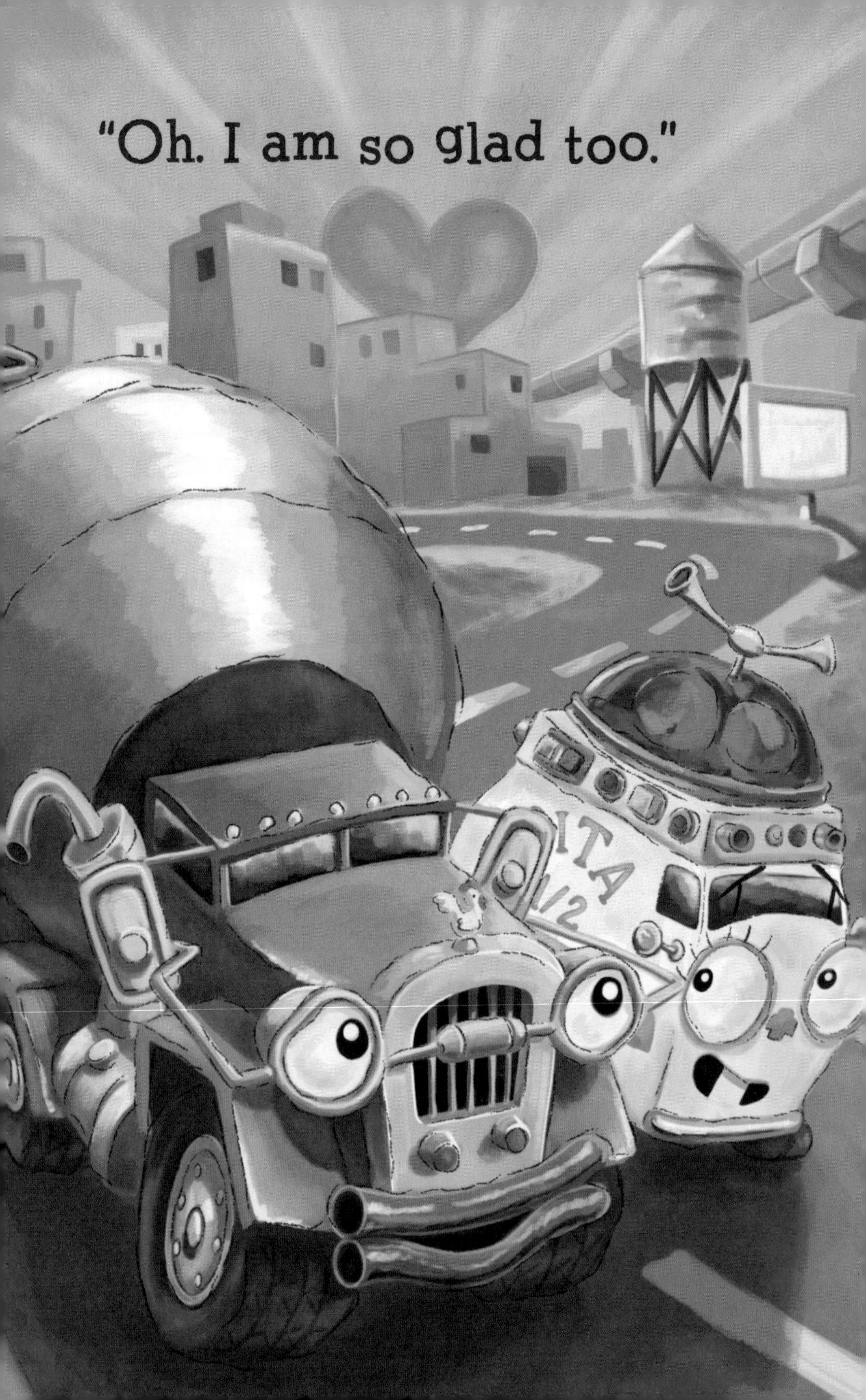